NEW FRIENDS FOR BOBO

THE • **BOBO AND IRIS SERIES** • BOOK 2

Words by **Celia Straus**

Illustrated by **Tina Salvesen**

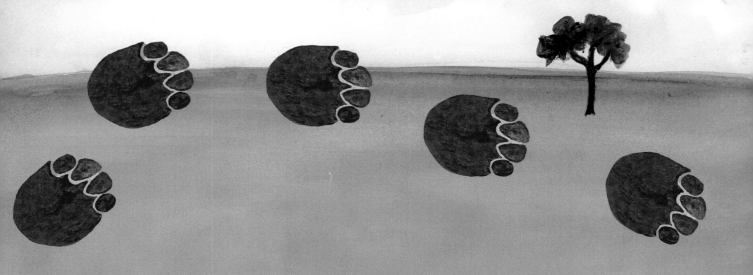

Reach Celia Straus
Instagram @CeliaStraus
Website www.zoerose.us

Reach Tina Salvesen
Twitter @Tina_Salvesen
Instagram @TinaSalvesen
Website www.tinasalvesen.com
Website www.zoerose.us

THIS BOOK IS DEDICATED

to orphaned elephants
around the world

BoBo loved living at the elephant sanctuary with his friend, Iris and his new mommy, Kindani. But sometimes he felt lonely.

One day, Iris and Bobo were watching two baby elephants, Tabu and Pika Pika, playing in a mud puddle.

Tabu was bigger than BoBo and Pika Pika was the smallest.

Pika Pika climbed on Tabu; lost her balance and they both fell. They laughed and blew muddy water at each other with their trunks.

"They look like they are having fun, Iris,"
BoBo said.

"They are *having* fun," Iris replied.
"And the mud protects their tender skin
from the sun and bugs."

"Why don't you go play with them?"
she asked.

BoBo sighed, "They haven't invited me."

"They don't know you want to play with them,"
said Iris. "Go over and ask if you can join in."

BoBo slowly walked over to the mud puddle and stood there.

"*Say something,*" Iris whispered.

"Like what?"
BoBo whispered.

"How about, 'Hi, I'm BoBo.'"

Before BoBo could say a word, Pika Pika said, *"Hi BoBo."*

"How did you know my name?" BoBo asked with surprise.

"We heard your new Mommy, Kindani, call you BoBo," said Pika Pika.

"Also, everyone knows when a new elephant comes into our family," added Tabu. "We are all baby elephants who have lost their mommies just like you."

"Do you want to play?" asked Tabu.

"Maybe..." BoBo said.

"Don't leave me, Iris."
he whispered.

"Are you kidding me?" Iris flew up
into the air flapping her wings like
a giant butterfly.

"Play in the mud with a
bunch of baby elephants?
I'll stand and watch, thank
you very much!"

"Okay,"
BoBo replied.

Pika Pika reached out and gently
touched BoBo's trunk.

"Let's try playing together again,"
she said.

"*BoBo doesn't know that. He's new to our herd.*
Say you're sorry!" Pika Pika repeated.
And she stamped her foot.

Tabu swayed his trunk back and forth, sulking.

Finally, he said,
"*Okay. Bobo, I'm sorry I scared you.*"

"Tabu, say you're sorry
for scaring BoBo,"
Pika Pika told him.

"But that's how we play,"
Tabu argued.

BoBo stumbled over to Iris for advice.

"They want to be your friends," Iris said.
"Go back to them. Be brave."

Bobo waved his trunk at Iris,
"I already have a good friend over there."

"You can have more than one friend, BoBo," Pika Pika said.
"For little orphans like you, me and Tabu, friends are our
family. We are brothers and sisters to each other."

But it was too late.
BoBo was already climbing
out of the puddle.

"Come back," Tabu said,
"I was just playing around."

"I don't want to play with you!"
BoBo cried.

"Help!" cried BoBo, as he tried
to scramble out from under Tabu.

"Tabu! Don't be so rough," Pika Pika said.
"BoBo is smaller than you."

BoBo tiptoed into the mud puddle. Right away Tabu pushed him so hard that he slipped and fell over.

"Come on, let's wrestle," Tabu yelled,
and he climbed on top of BoBo.

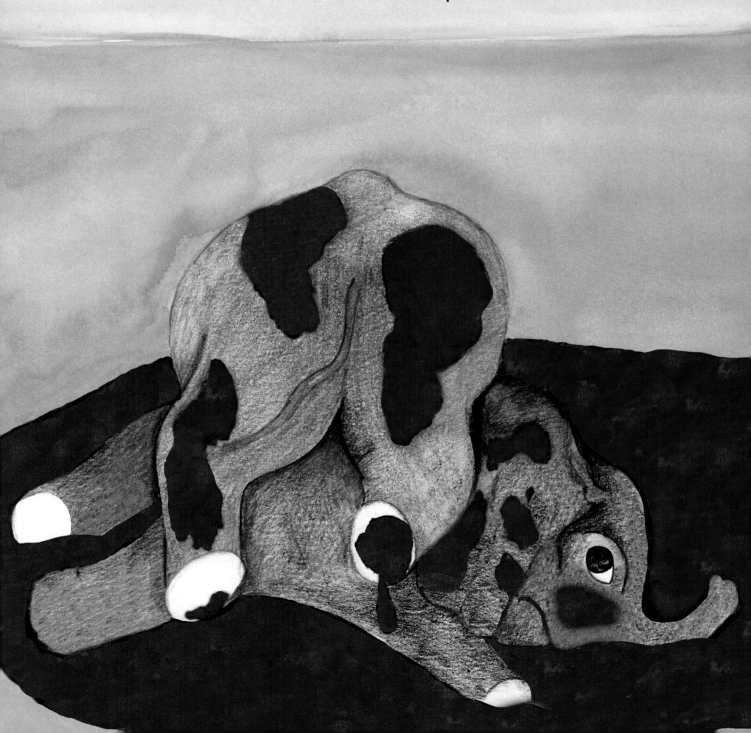

Suddenly he filled his trunk with muddy water
and showered Tabu and Pika Pika.

BoBo shouted, *"Look Iris!
I'm having fun with my new friends!"*

Sometimes it is hard to make new friends.
But BoBo finds the courage to try and discovers
what fun they can have together.

Look for book three in the
**BOBO AND IRIS SERIES;
BOBO LEARNS TO SHARE**